Jem Strikes Gold

Jem
Strikes Gold

Susan K. Marlow
Illustrated by Okan Bülbül

Kregel
Publications

Jem Strikes Gold
© 2019 by Susan K. Marlow

Illustrations © 2019 by Okan Bülbül

Published by Kregel Publications, a division of Kregel Inc.,
2450 Oak Industrial Dr. NE, Grand Rapids, MI 49505.

ISBN 978-0-8254-4625-2, print
ISBN 978-0-8254-7625-9, epub

Printed in the United States of America
19 20 21 22 23 24 25 26 27 28 / 5 4 3 2 1

Contents

New Words

canvas—strong cloth used for tents and sails

claim—a piece of land belonging to a miner

contraption—an odd-looking machine

critter—creature; animal

hit color—to find gold

jerky—meat that has been salted, cut into strips, and dried

molasses—a thick, dark syrup that comes from raw sugar

peddler—someone who goes from place to place selling goods

pester—to bother or nag someone

pouch—a small bag or sack

prospector—a person who looks for gold and other minerals

CHAPTER 1

Gold Camp Rules

"Hey, Jem!"

Jem did not answer his little sister. He was too busy.

A piece of gold was mixed up with the black sand in his round, flat pan.

A teensy piece of gold. Smaller even than the onion seeds he and Mama had planted in the garden yesterday.

But it was real gold.

"Don't bother me, Ellie," Jem said. "I have to get this gold flake."

He scooped a little water into his pan and swished the sand around. He was going to add this speck of gold to his pouch.

Even if it took all morning.

It might take longer than that. Jem's fingers were too big to grab the sparkly gold.

"Can I help?"

"Roasted rattlesnakes, Ellie!" Jem looked up. "You know panning for gold is a one-man job."

Ellie knew the rules. She was almost six years old.

Rule one. Stay on your own gold claim. *Rule two.* Pan your own gold.

Pa had a big gold claim along Cripple Creek. Jem and Ellie had two small claims next to Pa's.

"There's your spot." Jem pointed to where the creek splashed over five big rocks. "Go get your gold pan."

Ellie plopped down beside him. "I can't."

Jem sighed. He was nearly eight years old. Mama said he was the big brother. Big brothers must always be patient with little sisters.

Even when little sisters wanted to help every minute of every day.

"Why can't you?" he asked.

"Mama needs my pan to bake an extra pie for the miners."

Jem laughed. "You've been using Mama's pie tins again to pan for gold?"

Ellie crossed her arms over her chest. "They're just the right size for me."

Jem was glad his own gold pan was the real thing. Much too big for baking pies.

He went back to work. More water. More swishing. More sand dribbling over the edge of the pan.

Jem wished he had a pair of tweezers. Tweezers worked great for picking up teensy bits of gold.

Sometimes his prospector friend Strike-it-rich Sam let Jem use his rusty tweezers. Rusty or not, they worked just right.

But Strike was not here today. The old man had left three weeks ago on a prospecting trip.

Nobody in Goldtown knew where Strike went. Nobody ever learned what he found.

A new gold claim? A river where gold nuggets were everywhere, just waiting to be picked up?

Nobody ever asked.

Rule three. Mind your own business in a gold camp.

Miners never told anybody when they found a good spot. If they did, a hundred other miners would trample the claim and grab the gold.

More like a thousand other miners, Jem thought.

There were more than a thousand people in Goldtown. Most of them were men. Maybe only a hundred were women.

Mama was one of the women.

"So, Mama's baking an extra pie today?" Jem's heart gave a happy thump.

Another pie meant another customer.

Ellie nodded, arms still crossed. She looked grumpy.

Jem knew why. She wanted to help him.

After his third try at picking up the gold flake, Jem let out a big breath. "Wish I had a tweezers."

Ellie's eyes lit up. She dropped her arms and scooted closer. "My fingers are tiny. Tinier than yours. About as tiny as tweezers."

She waited.

Jem gave in. "Oh, all right. See if you can—"

"I can!" Ellie poked her head in front of Jem. She reached into the pan of wet dirt and sand.

Her thumb and finger pinched the gold flake. "Where's your pouch?"

Jem dug into his back pocket. Out came his wrinkled gold pouch. It held all the gold he had panned in his whole life.

The pouch was not even half full.

"Be careful," Jem said. "Don't drop it."

"I won't." Ellie squeezed her fingers tighter.

Jem held the pouch open. "Now, Ellie. Drop it in."

The gold flake made no sound when it fell inside the pouch.

No *plunk*. No *thud*. Not like the sound a big gold nugget would make.

Jem didn't care. Each tiny flake added up.

He pulled the strings tight and stuffed the pouch back in his pocket. "Thanks."

"Maybe next Saturday you'll pan a really big nugget," Ellie said with a smile.

Jem grinned. "Maybe."

There was always next Saturday.

Right now, though, Jem couldn't wait to tell Pa about his newest gold flake.

CHAPTER 2
Pie Peddlers

Ellie spied Pa first. She waved.

Pa could not wave back. He was carrying two big buckets of creek water. He set them down next to a long wooden box.

The tall end of the box sat on the creek bank. The short end opened into the creek. A handle stuck up on one side of the box.

Two rockers—like a rocking chair— peeked out from underneath the box.

The miners called the contraption a rocker box.

Pa and Strike were good friends. They didn't follow the pan-your-own-gold rule. When Strike was home, he and Pa worked on the rocker box together.

One person would pour gravel and water into the top of the box. The other person yanked the handle back and forth.

Water, gravel, and sand jiggled down the box and into the creek. The heavy gold always stayed behind.

Pa hoped to wash more gold with this new box than he could by just using a gold pan.

Jem would rather squat in the creek with his pan.

"Did you hit color?" Pa asked when Jem and Ellie ran up.

Ellie's head went up and down. "We sure did!"

"What do you mean *we*?" Jem held up his pouch. "I found a small flake and—"

"I put it in the pouch," Ellie said. "That makes it both of ours."

"Does not."

"Does too." Ellie put her hands on her hips. "It would still be in the pan if I didn't help."

Pa laughed. "Never mind, you two. Mama has pies for you to deliver this afternoon."

Pies! Jem had forgotten for a moment that Saturday was pie-baking day.

The miners looked forward to Mama's pies all week.

Jem's belly rumbled. Mama sometimes saved extra pie dough and some dried apples or blueberries. Two little pie tarts might be waiting for Jem and Ellie when they came back from their pie deliveries.

Yum!

"Let's go, Jem." Ellie headed for the large canvas tent their family called home.

Jem followed more slowly.

He wanted to deliver pies by himself. But the road to Goldtown was bumpy. It was also full of holes.

Jem needed Ellie's help. If she didn't hold on to the wagon's sides, it would tip over in the first rut.

That would be terrible!

"Hurry, children," Mama called. "The wagon is packed and ready to go."

Jem walked faster.

Ten pies fit in the bottom of the wagon.

Jem's mouth watered when he sniffed the air. Blueberry pies today!

"Bring back the empty pie tins from last

week," Mama said. She covered the pies with a clean, white cloth.

"I'll remember," Ellie said.

Jem nodded. "I'll bring back the pie money."

And maybe a tip.

Sometimes a miner was so happy for a pie that he gave Jem an extra pinch of gold dust.

Mama handed Jem a small pouch and a list of customers. "I'll have more pies ready when you get back."

Jem stuffed the list and the pouch in his pocket. Then he grabbed the wagon handle. "Bye, Mama. Come on, Ellie."

The pie wagon slowly bumped along Cripple Creek.

Jem left one pie with Henry Logan. Nine Toes took another pie.

The miners smacked their lips and paid in gold nuggets.

Jem dropped the nuggets into Mama's pouch and tucked it back in his pocket for safekeeping.

They walked farther along the bumpy road. Jem pulled the wagon. Ellie hung on to the sides.

Keeping the wagon steady was hard, slow work.

After a long walk, Jem and Ellie came to Goldtown.

Hundreds of canvas tents spread out everywhere. There were only two or three brick buildings. The wooden buildings had burnt down last winter.

Now everybody was living in tents.

Signs hung from the big tents. One read **CAFÉ**. Another said **GENERAL STORE**.

The biggest tent hung out the biggest sign: **SALOON**.

Some of the tents looked half burnt. Stovepipes poked up through the canvas tops. Smoke puffed out.

Jem was glad Mama kept their cookstove outdoors, far away from their tent.

He pulled the wagon to a stop in front of the café. "Mr. Sims, we got your pies."

A big man pushed aside the tent flap. "Just in time." He paid in gold and handed Ellie his empty pie tins.

Mr. Sims took a blueberry pie in each hand. He sniffed. "Your ma is a pie angel sent from heaven."

Jem smiled. Every miner in camp loved Mama's pies. She could not bake them fast enough to fill orders.

The miners and café owners had to take turns.

"Thank you," Jem remembered to say. "Good-bye."

Two more pies quickly found homes.

"Mama earns more money baking pies than Pa makes washing gold," Jem told Ellie.

He curled his fingers around Mama's gold pouch. *So why do I always feel like we are dirt poor?*

The answer to Jem's question stepped out in front of the wagon just then. "Hello, pie peddlers."

Will Sterling. The richest kid in Goldtown.

Will's father owned the new gold mine. Their family was building a brand-new house up on Belle Hill. It was the biggest and fanciest house Jem had ever seen.

Will always made Jem feel dirt poor.

Jem swallowed. Will was trouble too.

Big trouble.

CHAPTER 3

Pie Trouble

"What do you want, Will?"

Silly question.

Jem already knew the answer. Will wanted to pick on Jem and Ellie. He picked on them every Saturday afternoon.

Didn't that rich boy have anything better to do?

Probably not, Jem thought.

Only a few children lived in Goldtown. The schoolhouse was never full.

"What kind of pies are you peddling today?" Will asked in his know-it-all voice.

Jem and Ellie looked at each other.

It was not a friendly question. Will never asked friendly questions.

Before Jem could answer, a Bible verse popped into his head. *Be ye kind one to another.*

Mama expected Jem to be kind. Even to Will Sterling.

Sometimes Jem and Will said mean things to each other. When that happened, Mama found plenty of Bible verses for Jem to learn by heart.

He did not feel like learning another Bible verse today.

Will frowned. "I said what kind of pies are you peddling today?"

"Blueberry," Jem answered nicely.

Will grinned. "Mmm, I like blueberry pie. How about one teensy slice? You don't have to tell your mother."

Will was right about that.

Jem would not have to tell Mama anything. She would find out soon enough. The miner with the missing piece of pie would tell her.

"You can have a slice when your mother buys a pie." Jem tugged on the wagon handle. "Now, get out of my way." He paused. "Please."

"You are not my boss, pie boy."

Jem closed his hand into a tight fist. *Just*

one punch. One punch would send this sissy rich boy home.

"Jem, no," Ellie whispered.

Jem's hand relaxed.

A fight with Will wasn't worth it. Not today. He had pies to deliver.

Besides, Will never picked on them for long. He always said something mean and then walked away laughing.

But Will did not laugh and walk away today.

Instead, he stepped closer. He lifted the cloth off the last four pies.

"I think I'll just help myself," he said.

"No!" Ellie shouted. "Go away, you big meanie!"

Will reached into the wagon.

"Don't touch those pies!" Jem yelled.

Bible verses about being kind flew out of Jem's head. He pushed Will away from the wagon.

"Hey!" Will dropped the cloth and gave Jem a shove.

Jem fell backward into the wagon. His feet flew up. His backside came down on something warm and squishy.

Ellie gasped.

Will's face turned pale. He looked at Jem and didn't say a word.

Jem sat in the wagon. He didn't say a word either. He didn't move. His back felt wet and slippery.

Then Ellie began to cry.

Jem had to get out of the wagon and take care of his sister. That's what big brothers did.

Squish! Jem's hand landed in a gooey, purple mess.

He grabbed the edge of the wagon and pulled himself up. His feet touched the ground. At last!

Jem stomped over to Will. "Look what you did!"

"It's not my fault." Will's voice came out shaky. "I wasn't going to touch your sour ol' pies. I was just funnin'."

"You were not!" Jem shouted.

"Was too!"

Will turned around and walked away fast. "You shouldn't have pushed me," he yelled over his shoulder.

Sobbing, Ellie looked inside the wagon.

"The pies are smashed. All of Mama's hard work."

"Roasted rattlesnakes, Ellie!" Jem said. "Stop crying. You're not hurt, are you?"

She shook her head. Her two dark-red pigtails slapped her face. "But Mama's—"

"Look." Jem pointed near the front end of the wagon. "One pie is barely touched. We can sell that one."

He found the pie cloth and rubbed it across the seat of his pants. The cloth turned purple.

Good thing his pants were dark brown. Nobody would see the blueberry mess.

Ellie wiped her eyes on her sleeve. "Will's a big meanie. He didn't even say he was sorry."

Ellie was right. Will did not say he was sorry in words. But his white face told Jem he was *very* sorry.

Maybe even a little scared.

But probably not scared enough to stop picking on us, Jem thought.

"Come on." He dropped the cloth in the wagon.

Then he paused. The squished pies looked up at him.

Jem reached his finger into the goo and licked it. *Mmm!* "Try it, Ellie."

Ellie's tear-streaked face turned smiley.

She poked a finger in the pie filling and popped it in her mouth. "It tastes good. Not like a smashed pie at all."

"Pa says there's nothing so bad you can't make something good of it." Jem smacked his lips and reached for more. "Pa's right."

CHAPTER 4

A Sad Tale

By the time Jem got home, his lips, tongue, and fingers had turned dark purple.

Ellie told him so.

"Your whole *face* is purple," Jem said, frowning.

He felt sick inside. Not sick from eating the pie scraps. That was the best part of this terrible afternoon.

But . . . what would Mama say?

Jem did not have to wait long to find out.

"Good heavens!" Mama's hand flew to her mouth. She looked at Jem and Ellie.

Then she hurried to the wagon and looked inside. A choked sound came from her throat.

For sure she was counting the pies. Or what was left of them.

Her shoulders slumped. "How did this happen, Jeremiah?"

Jem's tongue felt stuck to the roof of his mouth. "I . . ." He swallowed. "I sat on the pies. I'm sorry, Mama."

"That mean rich boy pushed Jem right onto them."

Jem sighed. Leave it to Ellie to blurt out the whole thing.

Mama did not have to ask any more questions. Ellie talked faster than a chattering chipmunk.

When she finished, Mama sat down on a big stump and sighed. Then she held out her arms. "Come here."

Jem rushed to her. "I'm sorry."

"Me too," Ellie said.

Mama hugged them tight. "Never mind about the pies. These things happen."

Her voice sounded tired and sad.

"I guess I shouldn't have pushed Will," Jem said. "Maybe he really was teasing. Maybe he wouldn't have taken a pie."

He took a big breath. "He never has before."

"He mostly picks on us and says mean things," Ellie said. "Then he goes away."

Just then Pa walked up. He glanced inside the pie wagon. His eyebrows went up.

He looked at Jem. "Will Sterling?"

Jem nodded. How did Pa know?

"Cheer up, Son."

Pa picked Jem up and tossed him in the air. Then he set him down and ruffled his hair. "I know you did your best to take care of Mama's pies."

Jem smiled. Pa sure knew how to make a boy feel good.

The afternoon got better after that.

Ellie helped Mama clean up the pie mess. They piled the crust crumbs and the blueberry filling into a big pot.

Pa and Jem pulled the wagon to Cripple Creek and rinsed it out. Pa helped Jem wash his hands and face and the seat of his pants.

Jem shivered. The water felt colder than melted snow.

Later, Pa helped Mama load up ten more blueberry pies.

Jem eyed the wagon. He didn't want to

deliver those pies. Will might come after him again.

Pa's strong, warm hand squeezed his shoulder. "Want some help with those pies? I feel like taking a walk into town." He winked.

Jem's heart leaped. "Oh yes, Pa!"

Ellie stayed home with Mama, so it was just Jem and Pa.

Jem kept the wagon from falling into the ruts. Pa pulled the handle.

With Pa's help, they finished their deliveries in a jiffy.

Pa explained things to the miners who didn't get their pies. "You can come out to the claim and help yourself to what's left. No charge."

The miners laughed. "Aw, Matt, we can wait."

It was suppertime when Jem and Pa got back.

Jem was not hungry. Ellie probably wasn't either. They were filled to the brim with pie scraps.

But Jem ate what Mama gave him—a big piece of cornbread and a spoonful of brown beans. He washed them down with water.

"There's still plenty of light," Jem said after supper. He pointed toward the creek. "Can I pan for gold?"

"*May* I pan for gold," Mama said.

Mama sure was fussy about the way Jem talked. He sighed. "*May* I pan for gold?"

"Me too!" Ellie bounced up and down on the tree stump she used for a chair.

Jem rolled his eyes. "You gotta stay on your own claim."

"I will. I promise." She grabbed an empty pie pan.

"You may both go," Mama said. She looked at Pa. "How is the new rocker box working?"

Pa grinned. "It hasn't fallen apart yet."

He picked up his pan. "Come on, kids. Let's pan some gold."

Ellie grabbed Pa's hand and skipped beside him. Jem ran ahead.

Their gold claims were not far. Pa could throw a rock from their tent and hit them.

Strike's claim sat next to the Coulters' claims. It looked lonely without the friendly miner and his donkey.

Another miner, Pearly Teeth, was digging a big hole on the other side of Pa's claim.

"You never know when you might hit color in one of these," he said to Jem.

A shovelful of dirt went flying.

Jem jumped out of the way. *Rule four.* Watch out for coyote holes.

Coyote holes were not full of coyotes. Most of them were not full of gold either.

The miners kept on digging. They dug holes all over the place.

But they never found much gold.

"Yoo-hoo, Strike!" Pa hollered. "You're back."

Jem pulled his gaze away from Pearly Teeth's newest coyote hole.

He whooped. Strike-it-rich Sam was home!

CHAPTER 5

Strike's Surprise

Jem dropped his gold pan next to the creek. It clattered against the rocks. Panning for gold could wait.

Jem wanted to greet his friend. "Howdy, Strike!" he called.

"Howdy!" Strike tipped a bucket into the rocker box. He grabbed the handle and yanked.

Sand and gravel rattled down the box. Water swished.

A loud *hee-haw* added to the racket.

Would Strike's grumpy donkey let Jem pet him today? Or would it bite him?

Jem was never sure.

Ellie threw her arms around the donkey's neck. "I missed you, Canary."

Hee-haw! Canary never bit or kicked Ellie.

Jem stayed away from the donkey. He ran past Strike's small tent and headed for the rocker box.

Pa followed a few steps behind Jem. "Did you have a good trip?"

Strike nodded and kept rocking the box.

Jem skidded to a stop next to the old prospector. "Where did you go?" he asked. "Did you strike it rich?"

Ellie ran up. "How much gold did you find?"

"Did you find a big nugget?" Jem asked.

Pa shook his head. "You two know better than to pester Strike with questions."

Oops! Jem had forgotten *rule three*. Mind your own business in a gold camp.

Strike grinned at Jem and Ellie. "I didn't strike gold this time, young'uns. But I did find a different kind of nugget."

The miner jabbed a thumb behind his shoulder. "Go take a look."

Jem wrinkled his forehead. A different kind of nugget? Gold was gold. How could gold nuggets be different?

Unless Strike meant he'd found fool's gold.

"Aw, Strike!" Jem blew out a breath.

Would their miner friend tease them about a worthless chunk of fool's gold?

"Go on." Strike winked and pointed.

Jem turned around. A dirty-gold *something* lay under a tall pine tree.

He squinted. "What is it?"

The something moved.

Jem's eyes opened wide. It was an animal. He took off running for it.

Ellie got there first. She stopped under the tree. "It's a dog!"

She squealed and raced back to Pa. "Can we keep him, Pa? Can we? Please?"

Jem let Ellie do all the talking. He sat down next to the heap of scruffy fur, sticky burrs, and dried mud. "You're sure messy."

At Jem's voice, the dog lifted his head. His tail thumped. He rose and whined a greeting.

Jem scratched behind the floppy ears. "I bet under all the mud and weeds, you're golden."

The dog nosed Jem's hand and licked it.

A thrill went through Jem. *I want this dog.* He didn't say those words out loud.

A dog was not like a pet raccoon or a wild turkey chick. The animals Jem and Ellie found could take care of themselves.

A dog would need to be fed.

Jem peeked over his shoulder. Ellie had grabbed Pa's hand and was dragging him closer.

Strike followed. A big grin showed through his raggedy beard.

Pa was *not* smiling. He stepped under the tree and looked down at Jem and the dog. He didn't say a word.

He didn't have to. Ellie was still talking.

"I would brush him and pick out every burr, Pa. He could sleep next to me. He would keep me warm when it rains. And then—"

"Ellianna."

Ellie stopped talking. She looked at Jem. Her light-brown eyes were shining.

Ellie wanted the dog too.

Strike laughed. "That little gal of yours can talk the hind leg off a mule."

"Her mother and I are working on that," Pa said, ruffling Ellie's hair.

Ellie ducked her head.

"You young'uns want to hear how I found this critter?"

"I do," Jem said. He petted the dog.

Ellie nodded but didn't look up.

Strike squatted beside Jem. "I was prospecting way over by Jasper Creek. The third night out, this half-grown dog trotted into camp. He musta heard Canary."

Jem grinned. The whole mountainside could hear Strike's donkey when he *hee-hawed*. "Where did he come from?"

"I got no idea." Strike picked a burr from the dog's fur. "It looked like he'd been on his own for quite a spell. I tossed him some jerky-meat, and now I can't get rid of him."

The miner shrugged. "Hungriest critter I ever saw. I couldn't leave him behind to starve."

"Poor thing," Ellie whispered, stroking the dog's head.

Jem sank his fingers into the dirty, matted fur. He could feel the dog's sharp ribs.

Poor thing is right!

Jem wanted this dog more than anything in the world.

More than all the blueberry pie he could eat. More than all the gold in his pouch.

He sighed. Mama and Pa would not let him keep a hungry dog. Not when Jem and Ellie were hungry sometimes.

It would do no good to ask.

CHAPTER 6

Whose Dog?

"You may play with the dog," Pa told Jem and Ellie. "But don't forget he belongs to Strike."

"Hold on!" Strike said. "A dog needs young'uns to romp with, not an old-timer like me."

Hurrah for Strike!

Please let Pa say yes, Jem prayed with all his heart.

"Nope," Pa said right away.

Jem slumped. *God sure said no fast.*

Pa tucked his gold pan under his arm. "Did you hear me, Jeremiah?"

When Pa called Jem by his full name, he meant business. "Yes, Pa."

Ellie wrinkled her forehead. "But Pa! Why can't we have—"

"Ellianna."

She let out a long, sad sigh. "Yes, Pa."

Strike sighed too. "What am I going to do with a half-grown dog?"

Nobody answered.

"I can't get nothin' done," Strike said. "That pup sticks his nose into everything. Even my coffee. Nearly burnt his nose off this morning."

Ellie giggled.

Strike smiled. "It was kinda funny. He yipped good and loud."

Jem laughed.

"That critter is runnin' me ragged, Matt," Strike said. "I was hopin' you'd take him off my hands."

Jem held his breath. Strike was a grown-up. When he talked, Pa listened.

Most days, anyway.

"Young'uns and dogs go together like cornbread and molasses," Strike said.

Pa shook his head. "No, Strike." He turned back toward the rocker box. "You coming? Let's wash some gold before the sun goes down."

"Be right there." Strike winked at Jem and Ellie. "That dog will come in handy someday. He'll wiggle his way into your pa's heart. You'll see."

Jem wasn't worried about Pa. Pa had a soft spot for critters, just like Ellie.

"It's Mama who doesn't want a dog around," Jem said when Strike left. "And Pa will stick by her."

Pa and Mama always stuck together.

Ellie scooted closer to the scruffy-looking dog. "Why doesn't Mama like dogs?"

"I think she likes them all right," Jem said. "But a dog can't feed itself. Not like a wild turkey or a raccoon can."

"We could feed him leftovers."

"The chickens get the scraps," Jem reminded her.

Ellie sniffed. "I guess so."

Jem jumped up and whistled.

The dog barked. His tail wagged. He leaped after Jem.

Jem forgot about panning for gold.

He and Ellie splashed in the creek with the
golden dog.

Jem threw a stick, and the young dog
brought it back.

He was full of energy!

Ellie hugged the dog. "He's so smart!"

They played until the sun went down
behind the hills. Then Mama called them
home.

Jem took the dog back to Strike. "Thanks
for letting us play with him."

Ellie tugged on Pa's sleeve. "I wish we
could—"

"Shh!" Jem grabbed Ellie's hand and
dragged her away. "Don't pester Pa."

Ellie talked about the dog all the way
back to the tent.

She talked about him when Mama
helped with her nightgown. She giggled and
told Mama he'd licked her face.

Jem rolled his eyes. Ellie never stopping
talking.

Pa ducked inside the tent a little while later.

"Strike did that dog a good turn when he
brought him home," Mama told Pa. "I hope
he can keep him fed."

"Can we feed him, Mama?" Jem asked. "He's sure hungry."

Mama sighed and looked at Pa.

Pa looked at Jem.

"I'm sorry, Son," he said sadly. "The dog will have to stay hungry. You know how it is. Mama and I want to make sure you and Ellie have enough to eat."

Jem looked down at his bare feet. "I know, Pa."

"I know, Pa," Ellie echoed in a tiny voice. Tears dripped down her cheeks.

Tears would not change Pa's mind. Tears would only make Mama and Pa feel bad.

"Strike will care for the dog," Mama said. She held Jem and Ellie close. "Now it's time for bed."

She kissed Ellie's forehead. Then she kissed Jem's. "Don't forget your prayers."

Jem curled up on his cot. He pulled the quilt around his neck and closed his eyes.

Please, God, take care of that hungry, half-grown dog . . .

He fell asleep before he finished his prayer.

CHAPTER 7
Midnight Visitor

Scratch, scratch, rustle.

Jem's eyes flew open. His heart thumped. What was that noise?

He sat up and looked around. Most nights it was as black as a coyote hole inside their tent.

But not tonight. The moon was up. Pale light shone through the canvas ceiling.

Rustle, thump, thump.

Something was exploring inside the tent. A raccoon? A possum?

Two big paws landed in Jem's lap. A wet tongue licked his face.

Jem choked back a yelp. The dog! "Where did you come from?" he whispered.

The dog whined.

"Shh!" Jem hugged his neck. "Don't wake Pa and Mama."

He glanced at the bundle of quilts on the straw mattress. No one moved.

Ellie's cot was right next to Jem's. She didn't move either.

Jem's heart slowed down. He had to think.

The dog could not stay here. Even if Jem wanted to hide him, the tent was too small. Mama would find him in a hurry.

The dog had to go back to Strike right away. Tonight. Before Mama or Pa found him.

Jem pushed back his covers. He left the cot and tiptoed to the tent flap.

Tail wagging, the dog followed him.

Jem slipped outside and sucked in a breath. *Oh, wow!*

A full moon shone high in the sky. It lit up the cookstove, the tree stumps, and the tent in silver light. Not far away, the creek sparkled in the moonlight.

It was almost as bright as day.

Jem was glad about that. It made it easier to find Strike's tent. "Come on, pup."

Jem did not like walking over the sharp

rocks and dead branches. They poked and scratched his bare feet. "Ouch!"

The dog nosed Jem's hand. He held a stick in his mouth. He wanted to play.

"No," Jem whispered. He didn't want to play in the middle of the night. A chilly breeze blew through his nightshirt. He shivered.

Jem wanted to go back to his warm bed.

Whoo-hoo-hoo, whoo-hoo.

What was that? Jem peered at the dark shadows under the trees.

An owl flew over his head. He ducked.

Then he ran.

The dog dropped the stick and ran after him.

A minute later, Jem pulled open the flap to Strike's tent. "Wake up, Strike."

Strike didn't answer.

"Strike!"

Still no answer.

Jem let out a big breath. The old miner slept like a rock. Now what?

Jem yawned and looked down at the dog.

The dog yawned back and wagged his tail.

"In you go," Jem finally said. He could not wait for Strike to wake up.

He pushed the dog through the tent flap and yanked it closed. Then he found a string hanging down.

Quick as a wink, Jem tied the flap to the tent. "You stay in there," he told the dog.

Yawning and shivering, Jem ran home. His big toe stubbed a rock. "Ouch!"

He tripped over a pile of sticks. Would he ever get back to his warm cot?

At last Jem saw his family's tent. He slowed down to catch his breath.

His feet hurt. His big toe throbbed.

Jem crept under the tent flap and crawled back into bed. He snuggled under the quilt and closed his eyes.

"Jem?"

His eyes flew open. He rolled over and looked at Ellie. "What?"

"Where did you go?" she whispered. "I waited and waited. I was going to call Mama. I was scared you got lost."

"Lost?" Jem huffed. "It's light as day out there."

Ellie scooted closer. "I saw you leave. Something was following you."

"The dog."

Ellie's eyes opened wide. "He snuck inside the tent?"

Jem nodded. "I took him back to Strike."

"Why?" Ellie whimpered. "I want to keep him."

"Shh! So do I, but we have to do what Mama and Pa say."

Ellie sniffed. "I wish we weren't so poor. I wish we could find lots of gold. Then we could eat fried chicken every day."

She paused. "I would give some of mine to the dog."

Jem didn't answer. He was thinking hard.

His gold pouch was almost half full. Was that enough to feed a dog?

Maybe.

But I would have to pan lots of gold to keep feeding him, Jem thought.

"He doesn't even have a name," Ellie whispered. "We call him *dog* or *pup*."

"Strike will name him," Jem said. Then a new idea tickled inside his head. "Maybe Strike will let *us* name him."

Ellie smiled. "Maybe."

"Now go to sleep," Jem said. "Before Pa and Mama wake up."

He rolled over and closed his eyes. But he couldn't go to sleep. His head was full of ideas.

Ideas to feed a hungry, half-grown dog.

Mama and Pa would let Jem keep the pup if he could think of a way to feed him.

He was sure of it.

CHAPTER 8

Tagalong Pup

Jem yawned. He slumped over his bowl of hot cereal.

"What's wrong?" Mama asked. "Don't you like your mush?"

She held out a small pot of dark, sticky liquid. "I'll pour a little more molasses on it."

Jem nodded. He rubbed his eyes, sat up, and ate his lumpy mush.

The extra molasses didn't help the taste.

"Hurry, Jeremiah." Mama glanced at the sun. It was peeking over the hills. "You don't want to be late for school."

"No, ma'am." Jem finished the mush and picked up his books.

Mama handed Jem his lunch pail.

He looked inside. *Mmm!* A big piece of cornbread and a handful of dried blueberries.

"Hurry home after school," Mama said. "You can deliver the Sterlings' clean laundry before supper."

Jem didn't say a word. He stuffed his books under his arm and took off running for town.

He did not want to deliver laundry. He didn't want to go anywhere near Will's house.

Not after the pie disaster last Saturday.

Besides, Jem was tired. The dog had woken him up Saturday night and Sunday night. He was too tired to walk back and forth to town.

He couldn't tell Mama, though. She would ask questions.

Jem yawned. "I hope I don't fall asleep in class."

Miss Cheney would tell Mama. The teacher might even whack Jem's palm with her ruler.

Woof, woof!

Jem's foot froze on the schoolhouse steps. He spun around.

The dog wagged his tail. *Woof!*

"Oh no!" Jem groaned. "Why did you follow me? You can't stay here."

The dog plopped down on the porch and looked up at Jem. His tail went *thump, thump, thump*.

Three children ran up the steps and petted the dog. "Is he yours?" Perry asked.

"No."

"He looks like your dog," Ruthie said. "I saw him following you."

Jem let out a breath. "He belongs to my miner friend Strike."

Will walked up the steps. "He's a scrawny, filthy thing." He made a mean face and went inside.

The day did not get better. When the pupils sang "America," the dog howled.

The children giggled.

Just before lunchtime, the class recited their times tables. They chanted louder and louder.

The dog howled along with them.

The class laughed and looked at Jem. His face grew hot.

The heat spread to his ears when Miss Cheney said, "Take your dog home, Jeremiah."

Jem couldn't say the dog was not his. He could not argue with the teacher.

That was called *talking back*.

He had no choice but to obey. "Yes, ma'am."

Jem picked up his lunch pail and ran outside. "Come on," he told the pup.

Halfway home, Jem dug around in his pail. He took a big bite of cornbread and kept walking.

The dog whined.

Jem stopped and looked at him. "You're hungry, aren't you?"

Woof!

Before he changed his mind, Jem gave the dog the rest of his cornbread. "Don't tell Mama."

When he got home, Mama looked surprised. But she didn't ask any questions.

She didn't have to. She saw the dog and shook her head. "What a bother that pup is!"

Jem left the dog with Ellie and went back to school.

By the time school ended, Jem's belly was rumbling. A bite of cornbread and a handful of blueberries did not fill a boy up.

He kicked rocks all the way back to Cripple Creek. He wanted an apple or a piece of jerky. Maybe even a bowl of mush.

But Jem couldn't tell Mama he was hungry. She would find out that he had given the dog his cornbread.

So, Jem told his belly to be quiet. He ran the rest of the way home.

Mama stood waiting next to the wagon. Clean white laundry lay folded in a wicker basket.

"Make sure you keep the dirt off these clothes." She spread an old quilt over the top of the basket.

"Yes, ma'am." Jem swallowed a yawn before Mama could see it.

"Hurry back." She pressed a kiss against Jem's forehead. "We're having rabbit stew tonight."

Jem's mouth watered. "I'll be back in a jiffy."

Ellie stayed behind. Jem didn't need help with the laundry basket.

No sirree!

A quick run to town and back. And then . . . rabbit stew!

· ★ ★ ★ ·

Jem's footsteps slowed down when he got to Goldtown. His heart began to pound.

Will Sterling and his family did not live in a tent. They lived in a brick house on Main Street.

A cook fixed their meals. A maid cleaned their house.

And Mama washed their clothes.

"I wish Mama would stick to washing the miners' clothes," Jem huffed.

Gold dust sometimes stuck to the dirty clothes. Mama always smiled when she washed gold from the miners' clothes.

Jem took a deep breath and put one foot in front of the other. Will's house lay just ahead.

Jem frowned. That rich boy always made him mad.

He took a deep breath and prayed, *Please help me not to get mad at Will.*

Will was swinging on a rope. It hung from a big oak tree in front of his house.

When Will saw Jem, he dropped to the ground. "I'll take that basket inside."

Jem shook his head. He didn't trust Will.
Not one bit. "I need to get the money."

"I'll bring it to you." Will grabbed one of
the basket's handles.

"No." Jem's stomach felt sick. He grabbed
the other handle. "Let go. This is my job."

"These are my clothes." Will pulled.

Jem yanked.

The tug-of-war did not last long. Will let go.

Jem sat down hard. The basket tipped
over. Clothes and sheets spilled on top of
him. Some of the laundry landed in the
street.

Oh no, not again!

Will laughed and ran inside. He came back with the maid.

"Oh, dear!" she said. "What a mess."

The maid sorted through the laundry. She put the clean clothes in her apron. She piled the dirty laundry back in the basket.

Jem's empty belly felt tied in a tight knot. Tears stung his eyes.

Mama would have to wash the clothes all over again.

CHAPTER 9

Dog Trouble

As soon as Jem left town, he let his tears leak out.

He couldn't help it. He was tired, hungry, and angry at Will.

Why did that rich boy always make trouble?

Jem made sure his tears were dried up before he got home. He didn't want Mama to see him cry. She would be upset enough when she saw the dirty laundry.

He gripped the handle and walked faster. The wagon bounced over the ruts. The basket bounced too, but it didn't fall out.

When Jem got home, everything was upside down.

Mama was chasing Strike's dog. She flapped her apron and shouted, "Drop it!"

Jem stopped short. Why was Mama yelling? *Uh-oh.*

The dog had Ellie's shoe. He ran around the tent. He ran around the cookstove. His tail wagged.

"Come here, boy!" Jem whistled and slapped his hands against his knees. "Come here."

The dog ran to Jem and dropped the shoe at his feet. *Woof!*

"Good dog." Jem patted his head.

Mama ran to Jem and picked up the shoe. Then she saw the basket of laundry.

"Oh, Jeremiah." Mama's shoulders sagged. She looked tired.

Too tired even to cry.

"The puppy ripped Pa's Sunday shirt off the clothesline," Ellie told Jem. "He dragged away my best stockings, and then he grabbed my shoe." She sniffed. "Mama will never let us keep the dog now."

"Roasted rattlesnakes, Ellie!" Jem yelled. "Why didn't you take him back to Strike?"

He didn't mean to shout. The words flew out of his mouth before he could stop them.

"Jeremiah," Mama scolded.

"I'm sorry." Jem blinked hard. "I'm just so mad. Will and I had a tug-of-war with the basket. He let go and—" He ducked his head.

Mama could figure out the rest.

Pa came home from the creek just then. He looked at the pile of dirty clothes and sighed. He hugged Mama tight.

"Take the dog back to Strike," he told Jem.

Jem hurried to obey.

Supper was ready when Jem got back. He gobbled up two bowls of rabbit stew. He ate three big biscuits.

I bet the pup would like rabbit stew.

Jem did not say those words out loud. He didn't even ask if he could buy food for the dog with his very own gold.

No sirree.

Mama would not want to hear about the dog. Not tonight.

Maybe not ever.

· ★ ★ ★ ·

On the next Saturday, Jem asked, "Can I— *may* I pan for gold?"

Maybe he would find a gold nugget today.

If not, he could play with the dog. The creek was the only place he could play with him.

The golden dog had learned to stay away from Mama's flapping apron. He had learned to stay away from Jem's cot at night.

He was a smart dog.

Mama pulled three pies out of the big cookstove. "Yes, Jem." She smiled. "But this afternoon you and Ellie have pies to take around."

Jem's belly flip-flopped. "Can Pa go with us?"

"Pa has his own work to do," Mama said. "You always deliver pies. It's how you and Ellie help our family."

"Yes, ma'am." Jem scuffed the dirt with his boot toe.

Sighing, he picked up his gold pan and headed for his claim.

Jem spent the morning swishing his gold pan around. He found one tiny nugget and two gold flakes.

Ellie played with the dog.

When Mama called them home, Jem rinsed out his gold pan. He obeyed, but he did not hurry.

The wagon was filled with ten warm, dried-apple pies.

For once, Jem did not smack his lips. He didn't ask if two small tarts would be waiting for him and Ellie.

Instead, he bit his lip and took hold of the wagon handle. "Come on, Ellie."

Jem's heart pounded the whole time. When he sold a pie to a miner, he almost forgot to get paid.

All he could think about was mean Will.

Pretty soon, he and Ellie would have to go into Goldtown. Would Will be waiting for them?

Woof, woof!

Jem spun around. *Oh no!* "Go home." He pointed back to the creek. "Go *home!*"

Woof! The dog licked Jem's hand.

"Leave him alone." Ellie crossed her arms. "He just wants to see where we're going."

"He can't come," Jem said. "Mama will skin us alive if he jumps into the pie wagon."

Ellie's eyes grew big. *"Ohhh."*

But nothing Jem and Ellie said or did could shoo that dog away.

They were stuck with him.

The dog did not jump into the wagon. He didn't try to eat the pies. He didn't grab the clean cloth in his mouth.

Instead, he stayed close to Jem's heels. His tail wagged. His tongue hung out.

"Good dog." Jem stopped to pet him just as they got to Goldtown.

When Jem sold a pie to the shopkeeper, the dog sat down and waited.

Two miners bought pies and petted the dog. He licked their hands.

"Nice dog," one miner said.

"He's the best dog in the gold fields," Ellie said.

Jem grinned. He was probably the *only* dog in the gold fields. Jem hadn't seen any others.

"Come on, Ellie." He pulled the wagon around the corner. His grin faded.

Will stood in the middle of the dirt road.

CHAPTER 10

Gold Nugget

"Hello, pie peddlers." Will smiled. "What kind of pies are you selling today?"

Jem didn't answer. His fingers tightened around the handle. He would not punch Will.

Even if he deserved it.

Jem looked at Ellie. Her eyes were as big and round as an owl's.

"Don't let mean Will scare you, Ellie," Jem said. "He's all talk. Just ignore him."

He turned the wagon around. "Let's go the other way." He started walking fast.

Thump, thump, thump. Will's shoes slapped against the ground.

He caught up to Jem. "I don't want a teensy slice today. This time I'm taking a whole pie."

Jem scowled. "No, you're not."

Will grinned. "You can't stop me." He yanked the cloth away. "Apple pie! Mmm!"

"No!" Jem shouted.

"Go away!" Ellie's tears gushed.

Grrr. A low, scary growl came from behind Jem.

Will froze. He dropped the cloth.

The dog shot between Jem's legs like a golden arrow. His sharp teeth showed. He snapped his jaw and growled louder.

Will backed away from the wagon.

The dog sprang.

"No!" Will yelped.

The dog grabbed Will's pant leg in his mouth and shook his head. His floppy ears jerked back and forth.

Will shrieked. He kicked out his foot, but the dog held on tighter.

Grrr!

Will's face turned white. "Call off your dog," he begged, sobbing. "He's going to bite me."

"Here, boy," Jem called. "Come here."

The dog let go of Will's pant leg. Tail wagging, he trotted back to Jem.

Will's whole body shook. He looked at the dog. Then he looked at Jem.

Jem stared at Will. His thoughts spun. *The dog went after Will. He took care of us.*

Jem took a step toward Will. "Get out of here, Will, before I tell this dog to go after you again."

"Go away!" Ellie said. Her tears had dried up.

"This dog will be with us every Saturday,"

Jem told Will. "He'll make sure you never pick on us again."

Will shook his head. "I won't."

He backed up three steps. Then he turned and ran around the corner.

As soon as Will disappeared, Jem started laughing. He bent over and hugged the dog.

Ellie giggled and petted him. "You are the best dog in the whole world."

Jem and Ellie finished the pie deliveries without one mistake.

All ten pies found their customers. Gold dust and nuggets went into Mama's small pouch.

The wagon stayed clean. No smashed pies today!

Jem let Ellie and the golden dog ride home in the wagon. It was a lot of work to pull them over all the ruts and bumps.

Jem didn't care. He was too happy to feel tired.

"Mama!" he yelled when he got close to home. "Guess what happened!"

Mama stopped pulling pies from the cookstove. She stood up straight. "Jeremiah, get that filthy dog out of the wagon."

She flapped her apron. "Shoo, you—"

"No, Mama!" Ellie hugged the dog. "He—"

"He growled at Will," Jem said. He scowled at Ellie. "I'm telling this."

Ellie scowled back. But she kept quiet for once.

Halfway through Jem's story, Mama's frown turned to a smile. She looked at Ellie. She looked at Jem.

Then she looked at the dog. "Well, I'll be. I never would have believed it."

Jem dug out Mama's pouch. "There's lots of gold in here." He took a deep breath. "And I'm ready to deliver the next wagonload of pies."

Just then Pa walked up. He was smiling. "Look what I washed out of the rocker box this afternoon."

He held out his closed fist. "I struck it rich."

Jem and Ellie peeled back Pa's fingers. Two nuggets the size of corn kernels lay in his palm.

Ellie squealed. "Gold nuggets!"

Pa ruffled Ellie's hair. "Yep."

"The children struck it rich today too," Mama said.

"Oh?" Pa looked at Jem. "Show me."

Jem whistled. The dog leaped from the wagon and ran over.

Mama petted him. "He's a different kind of gold nugget, but just as precious. I could grow to like him."

"We can keep him?" Jem's mouth fell open.

Pa wrinkled his eyebrows. "What's going on?"

"I'll tell you about it while the children are bathing that animal." Mama dug through a box and pulled out a bar of soap. "The pies can wait. Scrub him good, Jem."

"I'll pick out the burrs," Ellie said. "My fingers are tiny enough to grab them."

Mama nodded. "After he's clean, I'll find him a bit of leftover rabbit stew."

"Mama!" Happy tingles raced up and down Jem's arms.

Pa put his arm around Mama's shoulder. "It must be a pretty good story if Mama changed her mind about you kids keeping the dog."

"It's a great story, Pa." Jem took the soap. "And I thought of the perfect name for him."

"What?" Pa, Mama, and Ellie asked at the same time.

"Gold Nugget."

A Peek into the Past: Gold!

Gold was discovered in California in 1848. By the next year, thousands of people had heard about it. They dropped everything and rushed to the gold camps.

Everybody thought they would strike it rich. The news reports said gold nuggets were lying on the ground. Or in the creeks and rivers.

You could just pick them up.

That was not true.

Most gold miners never struck it rich. They worked hard all day long. They worked every day but Sunday. Summer and winter. Rain or shine.

Many gold miners used a gold pan to find gold. They filled their pans with dirt, sand, and gravel from the creek bed. Then they scooped up water and started washing the dirt and sand out of the pan.

Gold is heavier than other minerals. When the sand and dirt wash out of the pan, the heavy gold stays behind.

Miners shook their pans and dipped the water again and again. Finally, all that was left in the pan were specks of gold, or maybe even a gold nugget.

It took hours to wash gold like this.

Many families made more money doing laundry or cooking than washing gold. Some opened shops and cafés.

They "mined" their gold from the miners!

· ★ ★ ★ ·

Download free coloring pages and learning activities at GoldtownAdventures.com.

Grow Up with Andi!

Don't miss any of Andi's adventures in the Circle C Beginnings series

Andi's Pony Trouble
Andi's Indian Summer
Andi's Fair Surprise
Andi's Scary School Days
Andi's Lonely Little Foal
Andi's Circle C Christmas

And you can visit www.AndiandTaffy.com for free coloring pages, learning activities, puzzles you can do online, and more!